D1156541

Topic: School   **Subtopic:** Numbers

Notes to Parents and Teachers:

It is an exciting time when a child begins to learn to read! Creating a positive, safe environment to practice reading is important to encourage children to love to read.

REMEMBER: PRAISE IS A GREAT MOTIVATOR!

Here are some praise points for beginning readers:

- You matched your finger to each word that you read!
- I like the way you used the picture to help you figure out that word.
- I love spending time with you listening to you read.

Book Ends for the Reader!

Here are some reminders before reading the text:

- Carefully point to each word to match the words you read to the printed words.

- Take a 'picture walk' through the book before reading it to notice details in the illustrations. Use the picture clues to help you figure out words in the story.

- Get your mouth ready to say the beginning sound of a word to help you figure out words in the story.

Words to Know Before You Read

crayons

friends

jackets

legos

pencils

tables

teacher

toys

NUMBERS
in the
CLASSROOM

Educational Media

rourkeeducationalmedia.com

By Constance Newman

Illustrated by Marcin Piwowarski

One.

One teacher.

Two.

Two pencils.

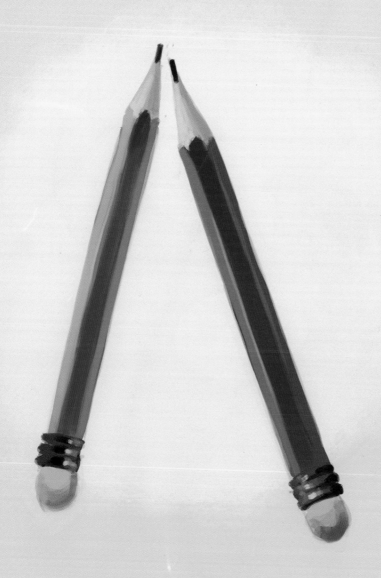

Three.

Three tables.

Four.

Four jackets.

Five.

Five toys.

Six.

Six crayons.

Seven.

Seven legos.

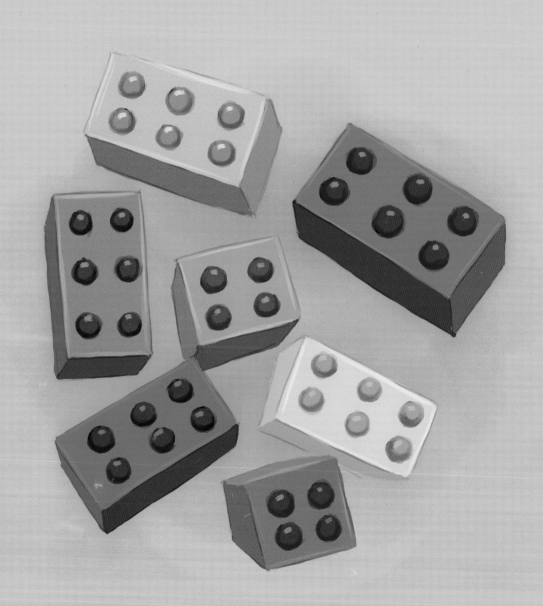

Eight.

Eight friends.

What do you see?

Let's count and see.

Book Ends for the Reader

I know...

1. How many friends did you see?

2. How many crayons did you see?

3. How many tables did you see?

I think ...

1. Have you ever counted numbers?

2. How high can you count?

3. What can you find in your classroom?

Book Ends for the Reader

What happened in this book?

Look at each picture and talk about what happened in the story.

About the Author

Constance Newman loves writing books for young readers. She often gets inspired to write by traveling to faraway places and seeing new and exciting things. She lives in Minnesota where the weather is often perfect for curling up next to a cozy fire with a good book!

About the Illustrator

Marcin Piwowarski is self-taught in traditional as well as digital illustration. He managed to make over one thousand books during his twenty-year artistic journey. As a single father of three kids, he understands what to include in his art for it to be adored and eye-catching.

Library of Congress PCN Data

Numbers in the Classroom / Constance Newman

ISBN 978-1-68342-697-4 (hard cover)(alk. paper)
ISBN 978-1-68342-749-0 (soft cover)
ISBN 978-1-68342-801-5 (e-Book)
Library of Congress Control Number: 2017935343

Rourke Educational Media
Printed in the United States of America, North Mankato, Minnesota

© 2018 Rourke Educational Media

All rights reserved. No part of this book may be reproduced or utilized in any form or by any means, electronic or mechanical including photocopying, recording, or by any information storage and retrieval system without permission in writing from the publisher.

www.rourkeeducationalmedia.com

Edited by: Debra Ankiel
Art direction and layout by: Rhea Magaro-Wallace
Cover and interior Illustrations by: Marcin Piwowarski